Praise for Storyshares

"One of the brightest innovators and game-changers in the education industry."
— Forbes

"Your success in applying research-validated practices to promote literacy serves as a valuable model for other organizations seeking to create evidence-based literacy programs." — Library of Congress

"We need powerful social and educational innovation, and Storyshares is breaking new ground. The organization addresses critical problems facing our students and teachers. I am excited about the strategies it brings to the collective work of making sure every student has an equal chance in life."
— Teach For America

"It's the perfect idea. There's really nothing like this. I mean, wow, this will be a wonderful experience for young people." — Andrea Davis Pinkney, Executive Director, Scholastic

"Reading for meaning opens opportunities for a lifetime of learning. Providing emerging readers with engaging texts that are designed to offer both challenges and support for each individual will improve their lives for years to come. Storyshares is a wonderful start."
— David Rose, Co-founder of CAST & UDL

Storyshares presents

Storyshares
Storyshares, LLC
24 N. Bryn Mawr Avenue #340
Bryn Mawr, PA 19010-3304
www.storyshares.org

Inspiring reading with a new kind of book.

A New Place Called Home copyright 2024 Sheridah Libby-Kuisch
Interest Level: Middle School   Grade Level Equivalent: 2.7

A Ten Dollar Bill copyright 2024 Jack Cole
Interest Level: Middle School   Grade Level Equivalent: 3.4

Lost Time copyright 2024 Elliot Childs
Interest Level: Late Elementary   Grade Level Equivalent: 2.6

Treasure Wasting Away copyright 2024 Theodore Henning
Interest Level: Middle School   Grade Level Equivalent: 4.8

Solu Soliga copyright 2024 Gajinder Kaur
Interest Level: Late Elementary   Grade Level Equivalent: 2.7

Book design by Saskia Globig

Adventures of the Heart

stories of courage and compassion

Storyshares

Contents

A New Place Called Home

Sheridah Libby-Kuisch

CHAPTER 1
The New Place

And there it is: the small, wooden house. Their new home.

It's surrounded by a lot of gliricidia trees and tall elephant grass. A couple of great kiskadees are flying around while the house wrens and pale-breasted thrushes twitter in the big trees. A woodpecker searches for worms and insects in the trunk of the mango tree. And a couple of chickens are watching the newly arrived creatures in the car on their ground.

"So, this is it. Our new home," says the keen dad. "Are you guys excited?"

"Yay!" says Mom. "This is going to be so much fun."

She opens the front door and steps out of the car. Dad opens the back door for the toddler and gets him out of his car seat.

"Mommy!" The little boy runs to his mom with his teddy bear in his arms. They both take a walk in the big, untended yard.

But there is another child in the back seat of the car. The teenage daughter.

She does not open her door. She doesn't even want to come out of the car. With folded arms, a sour face, and an unwilling heart, she looks out of the window.

Will you look at that little brat? she thinks to herself while she watches her little brother run around with his teddy bear.

Knock, knock, knock. She hears tapping on her window. Her dad is standing there. He motions for her to lower the window.

"You know, it would be much more fun if you would step out of the car and join us," he says.

"No, I'm staying here," she says, feeling annoyed.

"So, you're going to stay here day and night? 'Til tomorrow morning?" Dad asks. "Are you sure you want to do that?"

"Yes, I'll stay in the car forever," she says.

"Okay, suit yourself. With all sorts of noises

outside at night? Maybe a jaguar or an anteater will come to visit you," he teases her.

"You're lying, Dad!" she says. "That's not funny."

"Well, those animals are here, you know, in the woods across from us. Some neighbors have had visits from them at night, so yeah...." Dad scratches his head and says, "Listen, kiddo, I know you wanted to stay in the city close to your friends. But please try to give this place a chance? You might love it."

"I could have stayed with Aunt Vera. At least she's closer to the city. But no, you and Mom had to bring me," she grumbles. "You know it would've been so much better if you only brought Mason with you. Look how happy he is. Would've been a great pleasure."

Dad ignores her angry outburst. Instead, he opens the door.

He takes her hand in his hands, looks her in the eyes, and says lovingly, "You complain too much, sweetie. Yes, your friends are not around the block anymore. Yes, that means no more sleepovers and parties. At least, not as many, and not with your city friends. But you know what, Belle, you can make new friends here. Besides that, look at all the nature around us. You can take pictures with that new camera of yours."

"I don't know, Dad," she says quietly, knowing that her father is right. "I just miss my friends."

"I know," he says. "I understand. Come on, let's go inside."

CHAPTER 2

The Disappointment

Standing in the kitchen, Belle tries not to have another outburst, but her thoughts and feelings are overwhelming. Although Mom and Dad had already told her the house was old and needed some renovation and cleaning, she did not expect this.

There is a musty smell hanging over the whole house. Some of the beams of the walls are loose. The old paint is peeling off the walls. Dust is everywhere. Spiderwebs are in most of the corners.

It is a total mess. And it is a small house.

Belle feels uncomfortable at the sight of all of this. And she will have to spend a lot more time than she wants with her little brother in this little space. That makes her even more nervous.

She does not try to hide her unhappiness. "How are we all going to fit into this cramped, ugly, old house?" she growls loudly enough for her parents to hear. But she does not wait for an answer from them.

Dad built this house years ago, before he got married to Mom. After their marriage, they lived here for a while. Then circumstances made them move to the city. Now they've returned, and this time it seems like they're going to stay.

Belle isn't too excited about spending the rest of her life in this remote place. Not only is it far away from the life she's used to, but she had to leave her best friends behind. The house isn't even located on the asphalted main road. It's on a very long dirt road, where there aren't a lot of people.

She lets out a deep sigh and looks around.

There are pieces of wood on the floor. Old bags and a big, blue barrel take up a lot of space. Always the curious one, Belle wonders what's inside the barrel. She starts walking toward it.

Suddenly, she stops. There's a noise coming from behind the barrel.

Slowly, she keeps walking toward it. She jumps! Wait! What is that black thing running away from the barrel to the old bags?

She quickly picks up a long piece of wood lying on the ground near her. Carefully, she pushes the old bags aside with the wood.

"Mew... mew... mew." It's a cat! And it is scared.

Belle throws the wood down and drops to her knees. "Awww, poor kitty! How did you get in the house, little one?"

She tries to call the scared kitten, but it's terrified. With its little black ears pulled back and its black tail between its white back legs, the kitten tries to hide between the old bags.

Belle stretches her hand out to pick up the kitten. Mason runs to her, pushes her hand back, and picks up the little cat.

"It's my cat," says the little boy, while he strokes the crying cat on its head and back.

"Look, Mommy, my cat!"

He walks away with the kitten in his arms.

Belle is stunned for a moment. Did the little brat just come and take the kitten she saw first? When it dawns on her what just happened, she is furious. Angrily, she walks up to her little brother. He is still cuddling the kitten in his arms.

"Thank you, this is my cat," says Belle, grabbing the kitten away from him.

"Give it back! It's mine! Give it back!" Mason

yells, trying to take back the cat. But his sister holds the cat high over his head.

"No, dumbo," Belle says. "I saw it first."

"I'm not dumbo. Give me back my cat!" Mason cries.

"Dumbo, dumbo, dumbo. No, you can't have the kitty!" Belle says. She pushes him aside a little bit too hard. He falls on some pieces of wood and hits his head on the barrel.

Then Mason stands up, kicks her in the leg, and runs to his mom.

"Mommy," he cries. "Belle pushed me!"

"And you kicked me, you big baby," she calls after him. "It's my cat!"

"That was not nice of you, Belle," says her dad seriously. "You didn't have to push him."

"But I saw the cat first," she complains.

"But does that mean you had to push him? Or call him names?" Dad asks.

"But he kicked me!" Belle says. "Did you also see that?"

"Yes I did, but you are older and you know how to behave better than that. Go tell your brother you're sorry!" Dad says.

"But Dad..." she sputters.

"Go tell your brother you're sorry and give him the kitten," Dad says.

Belle storms out of the house and stomps to the backyard.

She finds her little brother sobbing in their mother's arms. When she looks at him, she sees a blue bump on his forehead. Was it from when she pushed him and he hit his head on the barrel?

Still angry, she grumbles a "Sorry" and puts the cat in his arms.

Immediately, the sobbing stops. He smirks in triumph! Wait, was he fake crying?

Oh, that little punk!

CHAPTER 3
Peace

Whoosh, whoosh, whoosh! Belle waves a thin stick in the air.

She is furious at Mason. The little brat has Mom and Dad wrapped around his finger. He is never wrong in their eyes. They never yell at him, even when he is disobedient. But because she is older, they always scold her for her bad behavior.

This is so unfair.

Whoosh! With one last wave she throws the stick into the elephant grass. A couple of startled lizards run away through the grass.

Plock! She kicks a pebble. It hits the trunk of the big gliricidia tree in the middle of the front yard.

It is then that she notices the swing on the tree. Sighing, she sits down on the dirty swing. Sometimes she wishes she was the only child.

As she slowly begins to swing, she watches two tiny, brown songbirds bouncing about with their short tails held up in the air. Sometimes they stop to sing a very bubbly song in the branches right above her head.

By chance, she knows these are house wrens. Back in the city, she loved watching documentaries about all sorts of birds, but especially the Surinamese birds. The house wren is one of her favorites.

Screech, screech, screech! She hears another sound. It sounds like the begging call from another bird.

Belle decides to find out where it's coming from and what bird makes that sound. When the two wrens notice that she's walking toward the old, dead tree trunk, they start singing more loudly. She notices it. She stops and watches them. Their behavior is a little bit off.

Screech, screech, screech! There is that sound again.

She follows it. It leads her to a hole in a dead gliricidia trunk in front of her. She looks in the hole, but it's too dark to see anything.

Though the sounds stop, she is sure they were

coming from the hole. The two wrens in the tree are watching carefully, still twittering away.

"Maybe there's a nest inside that hole. With eggs!" Belle says out loud. "And you two don't want me to take a look, right?" She nods to the wrens.

Belle takes out her phone and shines its flashlight inside the hole. Two big eyes are looking at her.

"A baby bird," she says. "It's a baby bird!"

Again, she notices the two fierce wrens in the tree. They hop from branch to branch and chatter very loudly to get her attention away from their nest in the hole.

"Hey, baby chick, are those two your momma and dadda?" she asks, smiling. She shines the light in the hole again. "Aww, you're such a sweet bird."

She takes a picture with the phone.

While she stands there and saves the picture on her phone, she suddenly hears footsteps behind her. It's Mason!

"Belle? Belle," Mason calls her. "Belle, are you angry?"

Mason is standing behind her with the kitten in his arms.

She looks at her three-year-old baby brother.

She had always wanted a sibling. And when he was born, at first, she was very happy. She played with him and loved being with him. But as he grew up, Mom and Dad always favored him. That's when she started to feel annoyed.

Now, her anger starts to build up again. She decides to walk away instead of being around him. But then Mason takes her hand.

"I'm s-s-sorry for taking your cat," says Mason. "Here she is." He wipes his snotty nose and holds the kitten out to her.

Although Mason is just three years old, he always says he's sorry when he knows he's done something wrong. He will try to make it right. And for that reason, she can't stay angry at him for long.

Deep down in her heart, she really loves him, even if she does get angry at him sometimes. She notices the big, blue bump on his forehead and his red eyes.

"I'm sorry too," says Belle. She touches his bump. "Does it hurt?"

Mason nods.

"You know what? Let's take care of this cat together! What do you think, Mason?" she asks.

His eyes brighten up. "Yes!" He hugs her. "I love you, Belle."

"Hey, you want to see something cool?" Belle asks.

Mason nods. She puts down the cat. She hears the bubbling songs from the house wrens in the tree, but she doesn't pay too much attention. She picks Mason up and brings him to the hole in the dead tree.

"What is it?" the boy asks curiously.

"Look inside." Belle shines in the hole with her phone light. "It's a baby bird."

"Can I touch it?" Mason asks. He tries to put his fingers in the hole.

"No, you can't. What if your finger gets stuck in the hole? Then Mom and Dad will scold me for that. So no, you can't. Besides that, do you see those two birds there?" She points at the wrens. "Those are the parents of this chick, and I don't think they would like it if you try to touch their kid. So let's not do that."

"Mew, mew, mew." The kitten rubs its little body against Belle's leg.

"Hey, little one, you also want attention, don't you?" Belle asks while she puts Mason down.

She picks up the kitten, but holds her back as quickly as possible when she smells her.

"Oh, eww, you need a bath! You stink!" She turns her nose away.

"I want to bathe her," Mason volunteers. He pets the kitten on its head.

Belle gives him the kitten.

"We need to give her a name," she says.

"Princess!" Mason says while he walks toward the house with the kitten in his hands.

"Princess Stinky," Belle laughs.

She decides to join her brother.

As she begins walking away, she sees the two birds flying to their nest. One of the birds goes into the hole, probably to see if their chick is still alive. The other bird twitters loudly, hopping around on the dead tree.

Belle smiles. She looks around.

There's a lot of green around her. Far away, she hears the howling from howler monkeys. Butterflies and dragonflies are flying around. She picks a pretty yellow grass flower. It's a dandelion. She smiles again while enjoying its beauty.

Maybe living here will be better than she expected. Maybe she should give this place a chance. A chance to be her new home.

A Ten Dollar Bill

Jack Cole

CHAPTER 1
Florida Storm

Fat drops of rain splattered on our windshield. We pulled into the gas station.

Most of the time, South Florida storms stop quickly. Today was different. Today, the sky looked angrier than usual. The rain did not stop.

The world around us was hard to see. It looked blurry.

It was so dark in the afternoon that it looked like nighttime. The wind was angry and shook palm fronds, branches, and leaves around us.

"We just made it," my mom said.

She pointed to the gas gauge on her console. It lit up in an angry shade of orange.

As my mother opened the car door, the wind knocked the door closed again. Surprised, we both gasped at the same time. Shaking her head, my mother laughed and pushed it open again.

I could see her fighting the storm to get out of the car. The door shut behind her with a loud slam. She struggled to get to the pump.

It was then that I saw him.

He stood about twenty feet away from us. He stood on the border between the storm and the gas station's protective overhang. His two-dollar poncho flapped around him, his hands folded under his plastic covering. He made sure he was far enough away from the pumps that he wouldn't bother the customers. This left him exposed to the biting rain.

His eyes closed for a few seconds. The driving rain covered his face and graying hair, soaking him from every direction. He was a large man, thick, with a brown-and-gray beard. I could imagine him as a fisherman or a truck driver or a miner, some-one who worked with his hands.

He leaned against a cement pillar, still and silent. He was the opposite of the noisy, messy weather that surrounded him.

My mother scrunched up her face. I wondered if her worried look was because of the storm, or because she was worried that the man would approach her for money. She said nothing to me as I watched her insert her credit card to pay for the gas.

A few cars were at the pumps around us, and the drivers finished before we did. We were alone with the man now, but he may as well have been in another city. He didn't even look our way. His eyes were set on the flooded streets around him.

Not wanting to stare, I looked at him briefly. I wondered how he had arrived at the gas station and how long he had been there. I knew I would never know the answers to these questions.

I watched as he stared out at his surroundings and I sat comfortable in my car. At that moment, I felt a need to reach out to him in some way. I wanted to let him know that the whole world was not as bad as the storm made it seem.

My mom finished pumping the gasoline. I motioned toward the man.

"Do you think I could give him some money, Mom?" I asked.

She looked at me and then at the man. She didn't say anything for a few seconds. I could tell she struggled with the answer. A few moments later, she nodded. She grabbed her wallet, pulling out a ten dollar bill.

"Is this a good amount?" she asked.

"That's perfect," I said. "Thanks."

Taking the money from her wet fingers, I push-ed open my door on the passenger side of our car. I put my hoodie up over my head. As I got out of the car, the storm had gotten worse. Now, the wind was so noisy it made everything around it seem quiet.

I walked over to the man and stopped about seven feet away from him. I knew I would have to scream for him to hear me. After a few seconds, he turned in my direction.

CHAPTER 2
Our Talk

I took a few steps closer to him. I tried not to worry that he might yell at me for talking to him or even try to hurt me somehow. I silently yelled at myself for what now felt like a really bad idea.

Second guesses filled my head. Maybe he was drunk or high or mentally unstable. But I was there, and he was looking at me, wondering why I was standing there. I stood about three feet away from him now. I leaned slightly toward him to hand him the money.

I cleared my throat and yelled against the loud rain, "Just in case you need this for something."

He smiled a grateful, sad smile. "You are a

special guy," he yelled back, as he took the money from my hand. "Thank you so much."

Without looking at the bill, he slipped it under his poncho and into a pocket in his shirt.

In his dark brown eyes, I saw that he meant what he said, but there was even more.

At first, it looked to me like he was hoping for a better life. Then, I realized I was the one hoping for a better life for him. I was the one hoping he had a warm, dry place to live in. I wanted him to be surrounded by friends and family who loved him. Mostly, I wanted him to have somewhere to go besides this gas station on the corner of a busy road.

Swallowing hard and unsure of my voice, I answered, "My pleasure. Stay safe."

I turned and walked back to our car. My mom was waiting with the car running and wipers on. The raindrops had found their way to the windshield even though we were under the awning.

She buckled her seat belt. "Ready?" she asked, as I sat down.

CHAPTER 3
Sunny Skies

I said nothing, but half smiled. We slowly made our way out of the parking lot. The only sound in our car was our windshield wipers swishing back and forth, trying to get rid of the water.

I turned back in my seat. The man smiled and raised his hand at me. He wasn't totally clear because the window was foggy. I waved with excitement and tried to blink away the tears in my eyes. At that moment, my only wish in the world was to change this man's life, so that he never had to stand there again.

As we drove home, the storm began to stop. Within forty-five minutes, the sun came out of the clouds. I knew that in a few more hours the storm would be gone. Only a few branches and puddles would remain.

I hoped the man at the gas station was warm and safe. I hope he knows I still think about him.

Lost Time

Elliot Childs

LOST TIME

CHAPTER 1

I did not want to go.

I had spent my entire life in Albuquerque, New Mexico. I had no interest in leaving. I had never been outside of my city, certainly not to a different state.

I had to go to Maine for the month of July. It was all the way across the country.

Mom was sending me to live with my grandfather after my grandmother died. I had only met my grandfather once when I was a baby.

"You'll love it," Mom said, "and you'll get to see the ocean."

Grandpa was in the navy. He loved the sea.

When he came home, he moved from New Mexico to Maine. Maine was where he met Grandma.

Grandpa lived in a town called Bristol, right on the water. I spent my time before the trip online, looking at photos of Bristol.

Pictures of rocky beaches and lighthouses and trees came up. It looked beautiful, but it was so far away.

CHAPTER 2

My plane landed in Portland. Grandpa was standing by his car. He was wearing blue jeans and a checkered shirt.

We said "hello" and drove north toward his home. A photo of him and Grandma was taped to the rearview mirror. In the picture they were holding me.

On the way to Bristol, Grandpa told me about what we would do. I could go swimming or hiking. I could look for birds or walk to a lighthouse.

I told him I was most excited to see the ocean.

"Good choice," Grandpa said.

45

LOST TIME

CHAPTER 3

Grandpa's house was small. He had a woodstove to cook with, a bedroom for him, a cot for me, and two big chairs.

Grandpa began to make us both sandwiches. I unpacked my bag. I was taking out my journal when I backed into a shelf, knocking it over.

Grandpa rushed over. I said I was sorry and sat down on my cot.

Grandpa knelt down and put books and boxes where they belonged. He saved the picture frame with broken glass for last. He put the bits of glass into the trash and grabbed the frame.

Grandpa stared quietly at the photo for five

47

minutes. It was him and Grandma on their wedding day.

"I didn't mean to break anything," I told him.

"I know," he said.

CHAPTER 4

The next day, after breakfast, we walked down to the water. The sun was bright, and the water shimmered. Grandpa wore a US Navy hat and his bathing suit.

"It's beautiful," I shouted when I saw the rolling waves.

I ran down to the water and walked in. It was colder than I expected, but I did not care.

I went up and down with the sea. I smiled at Grandpa on the beach. Grandpa took off his hat and came in.

After we got out, Grandpa put a towel down for me. The towel had Grandma's name written on it. The sand was hot under the sun.

"What was she like?" I asked him.

Grandpa sat for a minute before he replied. "She was wonderful. She loved you."

I looked back at the house Grandma and Grandpa had shared. Even from the outside, it wasn't much. Grandpa didn't like it much when Grandma was not there.

CHAPTER 5

The rest of the day was spent swimming in the ocean and eating the peanut butter sandwiches Grandpa had packed. By the time the sun started to set, I was very tired.

The sky turned from blue to pink and purple. I rolled up the towels. Grandpa packed up the umbrella.

Together we walked back into the house, which was the same as we had left it.

"Don't get sand everywhere," Grandpa told me.

I found my cot and lay down. The sheets were soft and cool, a welcome feeling.

On the shelf across from me was the same

photo of Grandma and Grandpa. It was the one I had broken. It still did not have glass.

"What can I get you?" Grandpa asked before he added, "To eat."

I hesitated for a moment.

"How about grilled cheese?"

"Sure thing," Grandpa said.

CHAPTER 6

We sat down with our grilled cheese sandwiches, and Grandpa turned on the TV.

"What should we watch?" he asked.

"I want to watch what you want to watch," I told him.

"All right, then."

Grandpa turned on *Law and Order*. He told me it was his favorite show.

"What's it about?" I asked him.

"It's... well, it's... it was your grandmother's favorite. We used to watch it together all the time. She always knew what was going to happen since she had seen so many. She would sit right where you are now."

I looked at the blue reclining chair I was sitting in. It had a blanket, knitted by Grandma, draped on it.

"I'm sorry. I wish I knew her," I told him.

"It feels like years since she's been gone. Almost forever," Grandpa said.

He normally looked so big in the tiny house, but now he looked small. The ceiling fan moved shadows all around the room.

"I wish I had more time."

CHAPTER 7

We did not talk about Grandma much after that.

We spent the rest of the month exploring the beaches and old lighthouses. They were my favorite.

They stood so tall against the rocks and the waves. They were a guiding light.

I ate all the fish I could before I went back to New Mexico, where we had almost none.

Grandpa taught me how to tie a knot and how to start a car. We used his kayaks and caught fish.

By the time the month was over, I was not ready to leave.

Grandpa drove me to the Portland airport.

Before I got out of the car, he handed me a red box with my name on it.

Inside was the frame along with the photo I had broken. He had gotten it fixed for me.

We said goodbye to each other. He stood outside of his car. It reminded me of when I had just arrived. I laughed when I thought of how scared I was to leave Albuquerque.

Now I have two homes.

Treasure Wasting Away

Theodore Henning

CHAPTER 1

"Your idea is crazy, Sunflower," said Tu'wu-da.

He used her English name rather than her Shoshoni Indian name, I'um-pi, which meant "sunflower."

"You are just scared, that's all!" Sunflower said.

"Yeah, maybe a little," he said.

"See, I told you, Tu'wu-da. The clan should name you different," she said angrily.

Sunflower had used his Shoshoni name, meaning "black bear." Normally, she called him Tommy Bear, but she wanted to make a point.

CHAPTER 2

They were the last of a handful of teenage Te-Mouk Shoshoni in that part of northern Nevada.

Their Shoshoni reservation had fewer than 200 people.

"A graveyard is not the place to go poking around," Tommy Bear said to defend himself.

"Bears are fearsome, strong, and able to face all challenges. But you, you are..." Sunflower stopped speaking.

She realized her words were not entirely true. To continue would not be right.

Tommy Bear was her best friend.

She knew he was brave and strong.

CHAPTER 3

Outsiders called her people Native Americans.

However, there was no getting around the fact they were considered Indians.

Shoshoni Indians.

Sunflower liked that better.

Yes, they were Americans, but every Shoshoni knew they were treated differently.

Most Shoshoni understood the treatment disrespected them. It hurt their pride.

"Scared!" Tommy Bear said. "Yes, Sunflower, scared." His voice brought her back to the conversation.

CHAPTER 4

"Remember, that graveyard isn't on reservation land!" Tommy Bear said. He shook his head back and forth. "That's Baxter Ranch property you are talking about. If we get caught snooping around, it would be awful, with us being tribal and all."

"Bear, they have secrets! I heard them saying..."

"Yes, and graveyards have dead people," Tommy said, overstepping her mid-sentence.

"But I overheard them speaking when I was at the trading post store on Highway 80. A white man said to the other man, 'It's a graveyard for treasure.' That's what he said, I swear it," she said. "He said treasure!"

CHAPTER 5

"Maybe so, but a graveyard is a sacred place. A special place for the souls of the dead," Tommy Bear said.

"Yes, I know. And it's probably even spookier with white-man souls guarding the treasure!"

Sunflower emphasized the word treasure by raising her voice.

Tommy Bear asked, "What else did you over-hear them say?"

"Well, as I walked to the end of the aisle, I heard their muffled voices. So I stepped softly around the end, but still didn't see them.

"All I heard was the white man say, 'It's a

graveyard for treasure wasting away.' And something about an old mine," Sunflower said.

"No doubt about it," Tommy Bear said. "That's Baxter Ranch property for sure."

CHAPTER 6

Tommy studied her face. "My father said the cowboys that work the fence line aren't friendly to us."

"OK, Bear, if you won't go with me, I'll just have to go alone!" she said.

"I'um-pi, do you remember when the other kids were talking about Father Amayo, the Saint?" he asked. "Did you hear the whole story?"

"No, not really. My mind was somewhere else during that dance," she said. "Tell it to me, Tommy."

"It didn't have anything to do with treasure, but it does deal with dead people," he said.

"So?"

Tommy Bear reached up, gently grasped her shoulders, and looked her square in the eyes.

71

CHAPTER 7

"We Shoshoni are taught from when we're young that burial grounds are sacred. Not only to the recently dead, but for our ancestors as well.

"We do not normally visit them. This is so we do not disturb their spirits. That is why we have ritual taboos. Why there are things that are just not done," he said, emphasizing the last three words.

CHAPTER 8

"I know, Tommy," Sunflower responded, "but I'm talking about treasure! Treasure in a white man's burial ground! I'm not afraid of spirits or their ghosts.

"Don't you remember reading the white man's story about Long John Silver? He was chief of pirates, and they took treasure wherever they found it! Graves included!" Sunflower said.

But she wasn't done.

CHAPTER 9

"Are Shoshoni rituals and dances done for the white man?" she asked.

"No, of course not," he said.

"And our taboos?" Sunflower continued. "They restrict we Shoshoni from disturbing ancestral burial ground. But do they extend to the grave-yards of the white man?"

"I'm not the one to ask, but I see your point. If our rituals and dances are only for Shoshoni peo-ple, then our taboos are only for our sacred plac-es," Tommy said, thinking about it more.

"But I interrupted you. Go on, tell me about

Saint Amayo," said Sunflower, now interested in the story.

"The kids were talking about that old mission northwest of Wells City," Tommy started.

CHAPTER 10

"They have a special burial spot in the mission gardens the priests call a tomb. The bones of Saint Amayo are believed to be buried in this tomb. Or that's the rumor."

Sunflower asked, "What was so special about him?"

"It is told he was one of the early Catholic missionary priests that came to Shoshoni lands a couple hundred years ago," Tommy Bear said. "He lived alone, but because of his strange ways he was eventually killed by our ancestors. To the Catholic priests, he is a martyr."

CHAPTER 11

"A lot of our clansmen were killed, fighting for our lands and way of life. Are they martyrs too?" she asked.

Sunflower knew her question didn't need an answer. She was asking it to make a point.

To any Shoshoni, the answer was obvious. Every brave that had died defending the Shoshoni people were indeed martyrs!

"The kids you were listening to?" she asked, looking at him expectantly with a slight bob of her head.

She raised her eyebrows. It was time for Tommy Bear to get on with the story.

"Well, it so happens that some of the young braves at Twisted Branch reservation accepted the rumor about Saint Amayo's tomb as a challenge," he said.

CHAPTER 12

"How could a rumor be a challenge?" she interrupted.

"I'm coming to that. The challenge part of the rumor is that if anyone uninvited were to enter the mission garden to visit the tomb, they could be captured by the priests. If they were captured, they would be made to kneel and pray inside the tomb until the daylight of dawn!" he said.

"So, these braves snuck into the mission, to do what? Visiting a grave isn't a bad thing, is it?" she asked.

CHAPTER 13

Sunflower thought about it.

"They could have tagged the adobe mud wall of the mission in the dead of night and satisfied their challenge."

"OK, Sunflower, you are a girl." Tommy shook his head. "Girls don't always understand things concerning us men. For the challenge, to prove Shoshoni bravery, they had to scale the courtyard wall, make their way through the garden to the tomb, and go inside."

Sunflower cocked her head slightly, giving him a puzzled look.

She asked, "Why did they need to go inside the tomb?"

"To steal Saint Amayo's bones!" Tommy threw his hands in the air. "They needed at least one bone or some of his hair for the talisman necklace. The bone holds the old priest's power!"

CHAPTER 14

Sunflower knew the tribal totems were sacred.

There was the claw of the bear, the feather of the eagle, the skull cap and teeth of the coyote.

These animals shared the earth with Shoshoni people.

As totems, they were also of spiritual importance.

The objects were reminders of their spiritual journey together in the great circle of life.

The challenge to steal an old priest's bones for a talisman seemed stupid to Sunflower.

"Yup! Those Twisted Branch guys really proved how brave they were. They got caught, right?" she said.

CHAPTER 15

Tommy Bear wanted to laugh out loud.

He knew it was a really stupid thing for them to attempt.

But he didn't laugh. He only let a smile and a couple bobs of his head acknowledge her point.

"And they prayed all night in that tomb!" he said.

"I know why you told me this mission story." Sunflower narrowed her eyes at him. "You think we, or rather I, would be caught by the cowboys and made to do something that would bring shame to our people," she said.

"Exactly, Sunflower!"

"Will you go with me and help me find the grave-yard treasure?" she asked.

CHAPTER 16

The next evening was the first night when all was dark and the moon was sleeping.

Sunflower and Tommy Bear hiked the country-side.

Tommy Bear had an idea of where the mine the men had mentioned was.

They both hoped the graveyard was not far away once they got to it.

Baxter Ranch property lay adjacent to the reservation, right up against it.

It meant they didn't need to expose themselves by walking along the road.

CHAPTER 17

Tommy Bear led the way. He was a good tracker with a keen sense of direction.

They crossed over gullies, around boulders, through scrubby, tumbleweed plant areas.

Occasionally, they came upon a cactus. Bouncing off one of them would hurt tremendously.

Yet Tommy led them to the fence without incident.

CHAPTER 18

Sunflower thought Tommy's moccasins had eyes because they had led them so swiftly in the darkness.

Passing through the barbed-wire fence was easy.

Once on Baxter Ranch land, butterflies filled Sunflower's belly. She recognized this to be the first sign of creeping fear.

Instead of letting it grow, she chose to remember the time she faced off with a wild coyote. It had snarled and stared at her, ready to lunge.

She had held her ground.

She had crushed any fear she had then. The coyote moved on. Now was no different.

CHAPTER 19

A few hundred feet inside the fence, they found a dirt road. Tommy Bear thought it led to the mine. In the still darkness, they followed it. They could see a light in the distance.

Once closer, they saw that it illuminated the entry of the old mine.

Being at the top of a tall pole caused the light to shine down upon much of the area.

That's when they saw it!

The mine went deep into the side of a hill.

The light pole was about 60 feet out in front of the opening.

No one was guarding the spot.

CHAPTER 20

Sunflower and Tommy Bear stepped out from the black of night and into the light to take a closer look.

"It's a graveyard, all right," Tommy Bear said, controlling the urge to laugh out loud.

"What are those things?" Sunflower asked. "They look like refrigerators piled up on each other."

It was hard to make out the shapes as the light faded into the darkness, but there could have been a hundred of them!

"Those, Sunflower, are old jukeboxes!"

"What?"

CHAPTER 21

"Jukeboxes," Tommy repeated. "Machines that make music. All the bars and country dance halls for the white folks had them. You put a coin into the juke and chose the song you wanted from a list. Then the machine played it. My father told me about them."

"But why are they here, all piled up like this?" she asked.

"You don't remember old Crow Feet, do you?"

No, she couldn't remember him. He more or less interacted with the young men of her village.

Tommy Bear was a couple years older, and that helped.

CHAPTER 22

Tommy Bear shrugged her off before she could answer. He knew she didn't remember the man.

"He had a Victrola machine. When the gasoline generator worked, his Victrola would spin a flat, plate-like disc called a record. Music would come out of the speaker on the machine."

"I don't know about records, but I know about cassettes and music CDs," she said.

Yes, times had changed, and some Shoshoni had embraced those modern changes.

Tommy Bear had carefully stepped out onto the edge of the graveyard pile. He investigated several of the worn-out jukeboxes with his flashlight.

He knew why they were there.

CHAPTER 23

"Sunflower, these jukebox machines are the old ones. These are the machines that spun those records. They were probably discarded when the machines using CDs came into being," he said.

"Well, why did that man call them a treasure?" she asked.

"I imagine, at the time, no one gave a thought to saving these machines. But... If one was working today, somebody might want it. Pay money for it. Whoever was replacing these boxes didn't think of that," he said.

CHAPTER 24

"I guess you're right," Sunflower agreed. "These were ordinary when they made music. There was nothing special about them. I guess people just tossed them in this heap to rot like bodies in a graveyard," she said.

Then she remembered the white man's words: "It's a graveyard for treasure wasting away."

Tommy Bear was right.

There was no treasure there that night.

Just old unwanted jukeboxes wasting away.

CHAPTER 25

Sunflower let out a disappointed sigh.

She turned back toward the fence. It was time to go home.

Tommy Bear went to follow her but stopped.

He looked at the pile rusting on the ground.

Before leaving, Tommy Bear reached in through the broken glass of one of the juke boxes and pulled out a flat, black record.

He quickly tucked it inside his shirt.

Then he headed to the fence line where Sunflower was waiting.

Solu Soliga

Gajinder Kaur

CHAPTER 1
Solu in the Jungle

Solu climbed up the tree like a squirrel.

He was very fast! He had been climbing trees since he was a child. Now he was ten, a big boy.

That's why Father had brought him here today...

Solu had covered his face with a cloth. Only his eyes showed. His chest was bare and he wore tatty old shorts.

"Careful!" cried Father from below. Solu was afraid to look at him, for it was a long way down!

He climbed up higher and higher, until he reached the honeycomb hanging tight by the branch.

The bees were very clever. They always made

their combs in places that were difficult to reach. But his father had taught him how to keep a lookout for them.

Solu would have to be very careful, or the bees would sting.

He lifted the handle of the comb very quietly while one hand still hugged the tree for support. It was small enough for him to carry alone.

As soon as he had it, Solu crawled back down faster than he had climbed up. In the last bit, he jumped off the tree altogether!

Appa slapped his back happily. "Well done, Solu, I'm so proud of you!" he said.

Solu smiled so wide, all his teeth glowed out of his dark face.

His skin was the color of dark coffee, shiny and brown. He had jet-black eyes and rough, black hair.

They hurried back to the *podu*. But before that, *Appa* offered prayers to the trees.

The Soligas always did that—offer prayers to nature—for she was always helping them find or grow their food. They prayed to the streams, the trees, the mountains, even to fire.

The Soliga tribe lived in the jungles of the BR Hills. The jungle was a very cool place, with lots of tall trees and shady branches. And lots of animals, wild animals!

Father carried the honeycomb, and Solu carried his big stick. They were very quick and very quiet.

They reached the *podu*. It was a clear area in the midst of the jungle. The trees had been cut off by their ancestors, who had made small huts of jungle mud, leaves, branches, wood, and hay. All the families lived close together. The *podu* had a strong, wooden fence to keep the wild animals off.

A stream ran nearby. The birds sat up in the trees and sang songs. In the rains, the peacocks would fly nearby and dance.

The air smelled so clean and fresh. Solu loved the jungle. He would never leave it.

"Look at what Solu found!" *Appa* showed off to *Amma*, pointing to the honeycomb.

Amma was happy for Solu, but she looked sad.

"Grandma has been bitten by a small snake. She is unwell!" she said. "Please fetch the doctor."

Grandma had been at the stream when the snake bit her foot. It was a small snake, but she was sick, all the same.

Appa went off to the edge of the jungle in search of the doctor.

Soon, he returned with Dr. Sudarshan.

"Let me have a look," said the doctor.

He checked Grandma's chest, eyes, and wrist.

He cleaned and covered the snake bite with a bandage and gave her an injection. Ouch! Solu hated injections! But it made her better already.

"Please stay for supper, Doctor," invited *Appa*. "It is *Rotti Parva*, the bread festival!"

"Sure!" said the doctor. "But I must get home before it gets too dark."

Dr. Sudarshan was afraid of wild animals, but not Solu! He had grown up in the jungle.

"Don't be afraid, Doctor, I will protect you!" he said.

Everyone laughed.

"Solu, why don't you go to school?" asked Dr. Sudarshan.

"School?" Solu asked. He had never been to school before!

"We have opened up a school where I live," said the doctor. "Other Soliga boys and girls come there too. They learn, read, play, or paint, or just sing and dance!"

Ooh! That sounds like fun! Solu thought.

"*Appa*, *Amma*, can I go too?" he asked his parents.

"Yes," agreed both.

"Good, then I'll admit him tomorrow," said the doctor.

Yes! Now it was party time!

Everyone came outside in the yard to sit in a

circle and share their meal. The Soligas always shared their food, but today was a special festival, *Rotti Parva*.

There was homemade bread, or *rotti*, and goat-meat curry. It was served on fresh banana leaves.

The meal had first been offered to the sacred Champak tree, which stood with a hundred stones at its feet. And now it was served to everyone present.

The women folk sang songs. The men dressed up in white lungis. They wore flower-and-leaf garlands around their necks and waists.

Solu's uncles brought out a cymbal, tambourine, and a drum to play upon. The rest of the men formed a circle-chain with their hands and danced. They bent their knees and twisted left and right, singing songs of their ancestors who had lived in the jungles before them.

Solu dashed in and did a spin-jump! He was very happy. It was a beautiful night under the shiny moon. He danced merrily.

Later, *Appa* and Solu walked Dr. Sudarshan home safely. They had a fire torch with them, so there was no need to fear. The animals were afraid of fire.

Tomorrow, Solu would start school!

CHAPTER 2
Solu Goes to School

Solu was so excited! Today was his first day of school.

He had gotten up early so that he could make it in time. School was just at the edge of the jungle, where Dr. Sudarshan lived. It was a long way off, but if Solu was quick he could make it just before 8:00, when school started.

Amma had given him a new white cotton shirt to wear. He had his blue shorts on already. He was not very sure about the shirt, for he felt very hot. But he wore it anyway.

He drank his milk quickly, without wasting any time, and said goodbye to his family.

"Wait!" said *Appa*. "I'm coming, too! I have to go pick wild berries and collect turmeric. I shall leave you at the end of the forest."

"OK!" said Solu. He was pleased to be going with his father now.

On the way, they stopped at the large Champak tree. *Appa* bowed down and lit incense. He offered prayers and then circled the tree. He told Solu to do the same.

"You must take its blessings, for it is the first day of your school," he said.

Solu was impatient, but he wanted blessings, all the same. He ran around the tree even more quickly than he could climb it and said, "Let's go!"

Father did not like Solu's speed, but they would be late, so he hurried.

At the edge of the forest, Appa said, "Solu, be good. Study well, and remember to get home before dark or the animals will roam free."

Solu nodded "yes" and ran.

On the edge of the forest was an open ground, with few trees and huts. Dr. Sudarshan lived in one of those huts.

The school was a large, brick house with many rooms. It said *School,* but Solu didn't know how to read yet.

He saw all the children standing in neat rows singing Soliga folk songs, so he joined them. All the Soliga children like him came from near and far to the school to study. They wore white shirts and blue shorts, like him. But they also wore white socks and black shoes.

Solu looked at his feet. He had never worn shoes, not even today. He had come with bare feet!

But this was it! Yippee! He was in school.

As the lessons started, Solu was asked if he knew any of the alphabet. He didn't.

He didn't know A, he didn't know B, and he didn't know C. So Teacher gave him a slate and chalk to practice ABC.

Solu found it so boring!

But then, he had chalk. He drew on the slate. He drew a balloon. It was flying off in the sky.

He loved balloons. *Appa* had taken him to the town fair once and bought him a red balloon. Solu had wanted to fly off with it into the sky. It was so light!

Soon, he filled up the slate with the things on his mind. And Teacher saw. She liked Solu's drawings. She gave him some paper and crayons. Since it was only his first day, he could draw for today.

Solu had never seen colored crayons before!

He scribbled colors and laughed with joy! He

loved the blue and red and green and yellow. And then he filled the whole sheet with beautiful de-signs.

Teacher was amazed! Solu was very fast. He was also very good with art. Teacher told him to go outside and do as much artwork as he wanted for today.

Solu drew and drew, until he finished all five sheets of paper. And he wanted to do more. But he had no more sheets. So he picked up the crayons and started to draw on the outer wall of the schoolhouse!

He drew and drew and drew some more, until the whole wall was full. And then he began to fill it with his colors. He had twelve of them! Red, blue, orange, green, black, and so many others, whose names he didn't know.

By the time school was over, Solu had covered the entire wall.

But what had he drawn? The jungle in which he lived.

His *podu*! His parents and his grandmother! And all the wild animals whom they lived with! Monkeys and birds in trees. Snakes and bison, deer and water buffalo. The Champak tree with its hundred stones.

His father fishing, his uncles hunting, his moth-er and aunts weaving bamboo baskets.

Even the fearful tiger, who roared out loud sometimes at night.

It was so beautiful, everyone came to see it in hushed whispers.

Teacher was surprised at Solu's talent and hugged him. She gifted him a whole new box of crayons and a whole new pad of paper.

Solu was joyful.

But now it was late afternoon. *Appa* had told him to get home before dark.

He told Teacher he must run off, and she let him.

Solu ran and ran through the jungle quickly, until he was safely back at the *podu*. He showed his gifts to his parents proudly and said he was now ready to learn alphabets!

That night, Solu slept with excitement and sweet dreams for his next day at school.

That night, the tiger, too, opened up its claws and roared out loud in the jungle.

SOLU SOLIGA

CHAPTER 3
Solu Meets the Tiger

Solu had been going to school for a few days now. He was very happy.

He had learned the alphabet and was starting to learn numbers. It was fun!

And there was always plenty of art.

Solu loved art. He loved to draw and fill in color, and he loved to paint with watercolors as well. Teacher gave him lots of paper to draw on as he wished.

But today, all the children had learned something new in school. They had learned how to make paper from sabbe grass themselves! Sabbe grass grew all around in the jungle. What fun it

125

was to make paper out of it!

Solu was skipping back home in the afternoon.

He now had black shoes and white socks to wear, just like the other children did. Dr. Sudarshan had gifted them! He was getting used to them, although they did feel tight and hot around his large feet sometimes.

Suddenly, he heard something pass through the bushes.

Solu stopped.

Again! And there was a purr!

Solu grabbed the thick vine hanging down by the mango tree nearby and leaped up in one jump. He was quick, and jumped on top of a strong branch.

The tiger came out of the thick trees and looked angrily at him.

Tiger!

Solu had heard it roar only a few nights ago.

Yes, there was an old tiger that lived in the jungle. It had been there ever since *Appa* was a child just like Solu, *Appa* said. But Solu had never seen it so close!

It was big, yellow with black stripes. And it showed all its sharp teeth to Solu. It was hungry!

The tiger growled loudly. It wanted to eat the man-child.

It was old. The deer were too fast for it. They ran away so quickly. The water buffalo were too strong for it. They always moved in a herd. But Solu was alone and weak. The tiger could hunt and eat Solu easily!

The tiger showed off its paws and sharp claws to Solu.

Solu sat without moving, but holding the branch tight. He would not ever go down. He was lucky to be up in the mango tree! Tigers couldn't climb tall trees.

The tiger circled the tree impatiently. Once. Twice. Three times. Then, as if to wait for Solu, it sat down under the tree. It was tired! Solu watched the tiger, with only his eyes moving.

Appa and *Amma* would be waiting for him. Would they know that Solu was in danger here? How?

Solu sat and waited. The tiger watched and waited.

Time passed by very slowly.

Only the wind moved the leaves.

Soon, it was evening. The sky was now turning red and dark blue.

But neither Solu nor the tiger had moved.

Solu's feet were sweaty. He wanted to take off his shoes. He wasn't used to wearing them for so long. But he didn't dare. The tiger sat right below him, waiting for any chance it might get to pounce at Solu.

And evening fast turned into night. The owls had started hooting. But wait!

What was that?

Solu could hear some distant sounds! They were coming nearer... It was the sound of their tribal drums and cymbals! And the sound of moving feet!

It was *Appa* and his uncles and cousins! They had come to find Solu!

Hurrah!

They came closer and closer. Solu saw the fire torches moving through trees from the top.

The tiger was getting nervous. It saw the fire torches moving too. It got up and shot evil looks at Solu, purring loudly. It moved here and there for a few seconds. Then, when *Appa* and the tribe came too close, it dashed away through the trees.

It was afraid! It had run away!

Solu cried loudly, *"Appa! Appa!"*

The men raised their torches even higher and saw Solu sitting on the tree. They had brought their hunting spears along, to protect themselves from the tiger.

Solu cried again, *"Appa!"*

He climbed down the tree and hugged *Appa*.

The others hugged him too.

"Well done, Solu! You did the right thing to climb up the tree and wait!" said Father.

"*Appa*, there was a big tiger..." Solu told them what had happened as he returned from school.

But the group did not stay there. They formed a line and moved quickly back to the *podu*, playing their drums and cymbals louder and louder to keep the wild animals away.

Solu reached home and hugged *Amma*, and finally took off his sweaty socks and shoes.

From now on, he would have to be more careful on his way back, but he would still go to school.

He loved it, and he loved the jungle, too. And he always would, even with all its dangers.

About the Authors

My name is Sheridah Kuisch (married Libby). Currently I am a stay-at-home mom. We live in Suriname in South America. A couple of years ago we moved from our place near the countryside to live on a dairy farm, further away from the country. Farm life is very challenging for me but most of my writing ideas come from my experiences here on the farm. Also my 7-year-old daughter's experiences are a great part of my writings. To me writing is a way to express my thoughts and feelings. As a young child I loved reading and writing and my dream was that one day I would also write a book. Writing for Storyshares brought me one step closer to finally see that dream getting fulfilled.

Jack Cole is currently a junior in high school. Winner of numerous Scholastic Art & Writing Awards (including the American Voices Award) and the *New York Times* Summer Reading Contest, Jack loves creative writing and strives to offer a voice to the day-to-day challenges kids face. He recently published *The Card Squad*, a middle-grade adventure story about a boy helping his grandfather who has Alzheimer's disease. When not writing, Jack is an ardent sports fan, a terrible basketball player, a passionate golfer, and an advocate for all furry (and non-furry) creatures. Jack currently lives in Florida with his parents and sister Morgan.

Elliot Childs, Theodore Henning, and Gajinder Kaur are contributing authors to the Storyshares library.

About the Publisher

Storyshares is a publisher focused on supporting the millions of teens and adults who struggle with reading by creating a new shelf in the library specifically for them. The ever-growing collection features content that is compelling and culturally relevant for teens and adults, yet still readable at a range of lower reading levels.

Storyshares generates content by engaging deeply with writers, bringing together a community to create this new kind of book. With more intriguing and approachable stories to choose from, the teens and adults who have fallen behind are improving their skills and beginning to discover the joy of reading.

For more information, visit storyshares.org.

Easy to Read. Hard to Put Down.

www.ingramcontent.com/pod-product-compliance
Lightning Source LLC
Chambersburg PA
CBHW051255170626
46809CB00004B/1660